Where are my Lambs?

You can read more stories about
the animals from Potter's Barn
by collecting the rest of the series.

For a complete list, look at
the back of the book.

Where are my Lambs?

Francesca Simon

Illustrated by Emily Bolam

Orion
Children's Books

1 3 5 7 9 10 8 6 4 2

Text copyright © Francesca Simon 1997, 2011
Illustrations copyright © Emily Bolam 1997

The rights of Francesca Simon and Emily Bolam to be identified as
the author and illustrator of this work respectively have been asserted.

A catalogue record for this book is available from the British Library.

ISBN 978 1 4440 0196 9

Printed in China

The Orion Publishing Group's policy is to use papers that are natural,
renewable and recyclable products made from wood grown in sustainable forests.
The logging and manufacturing processes are expected to conform
to the environmental regulations of the country of origin.

www.orionbooks.co.uk

For Ava

Hello from everyone

Mother Sheep

Baaaa

Tilly and Tam
the lambs

at Potter's Barn!

Mother Duck

Quack
Quack

Five Ducklings

Neigh

Trot the horse

Father Goat

Bleat

Billy the Kid

Honk
Honk

Gabby Goose

Woof

Buster the dog

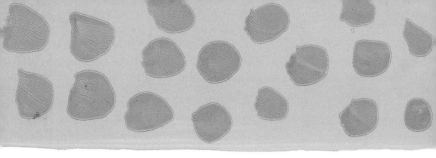

MOOOO

Daffodil the cow

Rosie the calf

Oink oink

Belle the pig

Cock-a-doodle-doo!

Red Roost

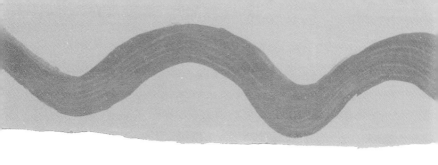

Squeaky the cat

Miaow

Henny-Penny

Cluck
Cluck

The chicks

Cheep
Cheep

Welcome to Potter's Barn!

The sun always shines and the fun
never stops at Potter's Barn Farm.
Join the animals on their adventures
as they sing, stomp, make cakes,
get lost, run off, and go wild.

The lambs were playing tag
in Butterfly Field.

"Got you!"
bleated Tilly.

"No! I got you,"
bleated Tam.

"Tilly, Tam,"
called Mother Sheep.

"Time to come in."

Tilly looked at Tam.

Tam looked at Tilly.

"HIDE!"

they baaed, and scrambled
behind the water trough.

Mother Sheep
looked to the left.

No lambs.

She looked
to the right.

No lambs.

She looked
behind her.

Still no lambs.

"Where can those naughty
lambs be?" she said.

And off she went to ask
Squeaky the cat.

"Baa Baa!
Where are my lambs?"
Squeaky leapt into the air
and did a somersault.

"Miaow Miaow!
With the cow," said Squeaky.

So off went Mother Sheep to
Silver Meadow to ask Daffodil.

"Baa Baa!
Where are my lambs?"

Daffodil the cow shrugged
her shoulders and chewed.

"Moo Moo!
I haven't a clue," she said.

"Very strange," said Mother Sheep.
"Wait a minute, what's this I see?
It must be my naughty lambs."

She crept up to the
hedgerow and ...

"Got you!" she cried.

"Oops, I've been tricked.
It's just an old tuft of wool.
Now where can those lambs be?"

"Ask Trot. He's sure to know,"
said Rosie the calf.

Off went Mother Sheep
to the stable.

"Baa Baa!
Where are my lambs?"

"Neigh Neigh!
Search the hay,"
said Trot the horse,
munching some oats.

Mother Sheep saw
something sticking up.
Could it be Tilly and Tam's ears?

She sneaked up and ...

"Got you!" she cried.

"Oops. A saddle. Tricked again.
Where can those lambs be?"

"Try the hens," said Trot.

Off went Mother Sheep
to the hen house.

"Baa Baa!
Where are my lambs?"

"Cluck Cluck!
Ask a duck," said the hens.

"Wait a minute,"
said Mother Sheep.
"What's this I see?
It looks like Tilly and Tam's
shiny black hooves."

She sneaked up and…

"Got you!" she cried.

"Oops. Wrong again!
It's just a feed scoop."

"Where, oh where, can those naughty lambs be?"

"There's nobody here but us chickens," said Red Rooster.

So Mother Sheep trotted to
Muddy Pond to ask the ducks.
"Shame I can't find Tam and Tilly,"
she said loudly.

"They were going to have a special
treat for supper tonight
… clover! But never mind –
all the more for me."

"Baa Baa!

Where are my lambs?"

"Quack Quack.

Check your back,"
said the ducks.

Mother Sheep turned round.
Her lambs were found,
safe and sound!

Baa baa
follow us

Did you enjoy Tilly and Tam's story?
Can you remember the things that happened?

What game are Tilly and Tam playing when Mother Sheep calls them in?

Who does Mother Sheep ask first about her lambs?

What does Daffodil the cow say when Mother Sheep asks about Tilly and Tam?

Who does Rosie the calf think is
sure to know where the lambs are?

What does Mother Sheep
find in the hay?

What do the hens say when Mother Sheep asks them about Tilly and Tam?

What looks just like Tilly and Tam's shiny black hooves?

Where does Mother Sheep
find Tilly and Tam?

For more farmyard fun with the animals at Potter's Barn, look out for the other books in the series.

Runaway
Duckling

Billy The Kid
Goes Wild

Barnyard Hullabaloo

Mish Mash Hash

Chicks Just
Want to
Have Fun

Moo Baa
Baa Quack